Charles Timothy Brooks

Roman Rhymes

being winter work for a summer fair

Charles Timothy Brooks

Roman Rhymes
being winter work for a summer fair

ISBN/EAN: 9783337256258

Printed in Europe, USA, Canada, Australia, Japan

Cover: Foto ©Andreas Hilbeck / pixelio.de

More available books at **www.hansebooks.com**

ROMAN RHYMES:

BEING

Winter Work for a Summer Fair.

NEWPORT, R.I.,

AUGUST 27, 1869.

By C. T. B.

CAMBRIDGE:

PRESS OF JOHN WILSON AND SON.

1869.

E.V.

CONTENTS.

I.

ROME DURING CARNIVAL (1866).

(A FREE SKETCH BY A MAN FROM THE FREE STATES.)

AND this is really Rome, as I've hearn tell of,
But little thought ever to see and smell of!
The place that all creation comes to visit, —
    Is it?
This is old Rome, — great Rome, the 'tarnal city,
  The more's the pity!
    By golly!
I'm glad I didn't bring along our Polly!
And this is the great Carnival I've been to,
And somewhat *into!*
As my poor powdered hat, and hair, too,
Can testify and swear to!
Oh! I've been knocked about from post to pillar
Till I'm as white's a miller;

And my old mop of hair, I vow, looks very
Much like a wax-berry bush in January.
This the great Carnival, I, ignoramus,
Once fancied must be funny, 'cause 'twas famous.
This really the Carnival, —
Where folks that used to be respectable,
Walking the streets at home,
Here, just because it's Rome,
And every man and every woman
Think they must be in Rome a Roman,
Stand up eight mortal arternoons,
Just like so many loons,
Or like so many owls
Filling the blessed air with hoots and howls,
And worse than that with stuff they call Confetti!
Tell that to our Betty!
She knows a confit from a pill, I reckon,
Or else I'm much mistaken:
     I should admire
     To have you try her!
You'd find a mess of fish grease in the fire!
Well, there they stand, each one before his *trough,*
Shooting the vile stuff off.

(Some on 'em in their rigs

Look almost like great pigs.)

I've seen a countess stand there by the hour,

And shovel down armfuls of dirty flour —

A thing ridiculous, not to say inhuman —

On every little baby and old woman!

I looked down on't from the top o' the house,

Where a man looks no bigger than a mouse,

And there, I own (not merely for a rhyme),

The *tout ensemble* almost looked sublime.

And when the troopers clanked along the street

And made that lane, the thing was done so neat,

They cleared the track so handsome, and much more so

The little dog that yelped along the Corso;

And when the little horses flew like lightning,

And all the faster for a little frightening;

And then, when they'd shot by, to see the track

Turn instantaneously from brown to black, —

It seemed up there a somewhat clean conclusion

To such a day of dirt and of confusion.

But here, a hundred feet above the people,

Having for nearest neighbors roof and steeple,

Did there not come to me that hour a feeling
Standing beneath my grand sky-parlor's ceiling, —
The blue Italian heaven looked never cleaner,
The green of Monte Pincio never greener!

———◆———

Second Blast.

P.S. — Since writing the foregoing ditty
(Before the Carnival had ended quite),
I have experienced a transcendent night
    In this eternal city:
I was about to call it — not *eternal*,
But by another word that ends in — fernal;
For, sure, this side the dismal regions
Where Satan marshals his discordant legions, —
Short of that dismal dwelling
Could scarce be matched the yelling,
The screaming, and the shrieking,
The howling and the squeaking,
That long past midnight sounded,
Confusion worse confounded.

Noise and nonsense joined their powers

Just to spoil four precious hours.

I thought in fact *that other place* were preferable,

For there at least the outcries would be referable

Each to some definite emotion ;

But here no creature seemed to have a notion

Of what he meant, except to make a racket,

Banging night's eàr-drum hard enough to crack it.

Hogarth's enraged musician,

Compared with me, was in a mild condition.

Sometimes they'd all set up a general screaming,

And then apparently deeming

Monotonous noise might soothe some wretch's slumber,

A certain (or uncertain) number

Would start some quick, sharp cries, that, ever madder

Flew up the invisible atmospheric ladder,

Where each one seemed to labor

To overtop his neighbor ;

And all the while that stony-hearted tambourine

Kept up its pound and jingle in between.

A hundred donkeys, each

Afflicted with a special influenza,

And his peculiar hee-haw, groan, and screech,

I could have borne *con summa patienza.*

To sleep, I was too crazy;

To fling a water-pitcher out, too lazy:

I was half-furious,

And yet withal half-curious

To know — was there a goal to this mad power?

And should I live to see the final hour?

Was my brain, or those rascals' lungs the strongest?

And which of us, perhaps, would hold out longest?

Towards two o'clock I fancied I detected

Some giving out, and confidently expected

The thing was coming to an end: next minute

It seemed as they were just going to begin it.

And then would come a sudden thunderation,

Threatening to shake the house to its foundation.

At last the smaller fry did seem to scatter,

And only the big bulls keep up the clatter.

A ray of hope was through my misery gleaming,

The yelling thinned away to roaring, screaming;

Then some kind neighbors (how the street should thank
  'em!)

With flute and fiddle made a move to flank 'em.

Then the dirt-carts, like an artillery rattle,

Coming to clean the Corso, closed the battle ;

And when the last vile sounds had died away,

How like a poultice * on the senses lay

That blessed silence ! —

More I cannot say !

—◆—

P P. S.

Having recovered some from that night business,

Though still affected with a certain dizziness,

A kind of haziness,

And general laziness, —

I own that evening of the moccoletti

Was very pretty,

And *that* I should have liked to show to Betty,

(Only she's dreadful 'fraid of spermacetty !)

To look along a mile of glittering alley,

Straight up and down a sort of mountain valley,

---

* Holmes.

And see, as daylight, and the horse-race, closes,

Each slope burst out a blaze of fiery roses,

And down below a fiery stream that flashes, —

Or fiery snake, I'll say, with some black gashes

(That's when the lights went out, the fellows carried,

Squelched by some blow that couldn't well be parried,

Making a sort of parenthesis in the glory,

As I do, in the middle of my story) —

As I was saying, it *was* a handsome go-off,

Though not so handsome, quite, as some I know of;

For instance, when the glorious Yankee nation

Get up a 4th July illumination —

Still it *was* handsome, that there's no denying,

Although to get to it was rayther trying:

    I had to rough it,

    And tough it,

And oh! my poor cheek-bones got many a buffet

From nosegays, *mostly stalks*, of moderate thickness,

Jerked by bold urchins with spasmodic quickness.

But there's no rose without a thorn, I know it,

And well my late experience goes to show it.

He that plays jokes must not mind being joked at;

He that pokes fun, no wonder if he's poked at:

This is a truth oft pressed on my conviction

During the recent Carnival affliction.

Didn't I wield my ten-foot cane-pole featly,

And douse the glim of many a chap full neatly?

And did I not, in an unlucky hour,

Bow to superior (say *inferior*) power,

When that bold man (whose name I have not learned
    yet,

Because the cane-pole has not been returned yet)

Caught at the rag below, (humiliation!)

And dragged my pole down, and my reputation!

Well, I am glad the Carnival is ended,

And carnal sports are for a while suspended.

Here for a while, too, I'll suspend my strictures,

And go to see the ruins and the pictures.

II.

ROMAN RUINS.

(DONE INTO WHAT JEAN PAUL CALLS "STRECK-VERSE," BY A
PARTIALLY INFORMED YANKEE.)

I SAID, you remember, when I finished that three-part
Pome

(As our Southern sisters say) about the Carnival doin's
in Rome,

As how I was going to suspend for a while my moral
stricters,

And go to see the ruins and the picters.

Well, I've been and seen some of the ruins,

And I'll tell you my private opinion: *them's somebody's
doin's.*

I haven't said it outright, but I've often said so men-
tally;

Them kind of things don't never come accidentally.

Some of the rubbish does, to be sure, look e'enamost
  like a part of Natur,
It's been so kivered over and dressed up by old Alma
  Mater;
But anybody can see, that ain't an impostor or an igno-
  ramus,
That men must have had a hand in it, and some that
  was pooty famous.
In the town where I was raised there was a feller
(I think his brains must have been considerably meller),
If you showed him them fossil things they dig up in the
  strater,
You couldn't beat it out of the head of that crater,
They grew there by chance; and sometimes he was so
  oncivil,
As jest to insinooate they was the work of the divil,
Who went and put 'em there to give poor mortal brains
  new trouble,
And blow up a great geological bubble.
— But, deary me! where was I? This Rome sets one's
  brain a spinnin',
So I must e'en go back and begin again at the beginnin'.

Well, one fine morning I went to a place they call the
    Propergander

(*Propergoose!* I reckon 'twould puzzle our Amanda

To tell what that word means), and hired a *Carrotzy.*

    (By jingo!

I never heard the beat of this Eyetalian lingo!)

'Twas rayther a dirty consarn, that carrotzy;

The lining faded out and the framework summat squatsy.

But I'm one of them folks as ain't very perticler,

Provided they only can get into somethin' vehiclar.

So we druv down through a long narrow alley:

How I wish *you* could have been there, cousin Sally!

To see the oranges, all golden-yeller,

Peeping over the wall to tantalize a feller:

Some pretend they're the bitter kind,—*yes*, no doubt,
    and sour,

As the fox said of the grapes when they was out of his
    power!

Anyhow they *looked* beautiful, and so did the roses

And blossoms and bushes, and various kinds of pinks
    and posies.

And, oh! if you could *only* have seen that cunnin' lizard

That shot along the wall quicker'n you could say *izzard.*

They come out on the side o' the walls to get a sunning;
But the moment they see anybody, they commence run-
    ning.
The little chaps don't stand much frightenin',
And they go it like a streak of green lightnin'.
Well, as I was a saying, we went down that long alley
'Till we came to a place called the Baths of Carrycally.
(That was the name, I think, as I heern 'em tell it,
But I'll be switched if I know how they spell it.)
You go in through a great garden-walk among cabbages
    and roses,
Lined with curus old stone faces, some without any
    noses.
The old feller that owns the place let us in through the
    garden;
He wears a snuff-colored coat, and in making a bargain
    they say is a hard 'un.
He's one of the Carrycallys, I believe, — one of the
    later branches;
At any rate, he's got one of the most extrornary ranches,
Richer than any, I guess, in the Mexican valley,
Has this old grand-nephew of the original Carrycally.

He's got a blacksmith's shop in old gran'ther Carry-
  cally's stables,
And there, spread out on ever so many tables,
He's got an assortment of broken legs, arms, and noses
(Marble, of course) ; and he puts 'em together as he
  supposes
They was meant to go, and sometimes he hits it,
And finds a piece that'll fit, and goes and fits it.
But when he finds one that won't gee nor haw,
He just throws it aside in the table-draw.
I thought to myself, as I looked at 'em all, I wonder
What the old chap 'd take for all that plunder ;
But I didn't dare ask him, for I've a fancy
His price would seem extravagant to our Nancy.
Well, he took us round among his excavations, to view
  'em, —
Dickens's Golden Dustman's heap was nothing to 'em.
Seventy feet down we looked, and saw things 'most
  superhuman —
Sich as, a horse with a dragon's tail, carryin' a woman —
A picter, I mean, on the floor of old Carrycaller,
All painted out to the life, in spots of black and yeller.

It must have dated back e'enamost to the creation ;

The man said it come down from the *Mosaic* dispen-
sation.

Then we went over to a great square brick room they
used to swim in ;

'Twas meant I s'pose for the men, there didn't seem to
be any for the women.

And close by was a *round* brick room, a large one, very,

Where, when they was scrubbed and rigged, they could
go in and make merry.

And high up agin the wall they showed us the traces

Of the gallery where the musical folks had their places.

I couldn't help thinking, as I looked at the walls, that
the brick work

Was uncommonly, and I should say, *unnecessarily* thick
work.

And when I thought of all the hod-carrying and brick-
making,

It actilly almost set my old bones to aching.

I don't know what sort of a man that old Mr. Carrycally

May or may not have been, but he don't seem to have
set much .vally

On bricks or bones, no, nor on money nuther ;

For it must have cost a heap to get all this together.

Well, I do hope he enjoyed it whilst he was living,

All that splendid establishment, without any shadow of
    misgiving ;

For a brick nightmare of that size, on a man's conscience,
    I consider,

Must, in the nature of things, have soon left his wife a
    widder.

But I find my muse is running into melancholy reflec-
    tions,

And will resume another time in some pleasanter direc-
    tions.

III.

THE BALL OF ST. PETER'S.

THAT last poem of mine gave my friends so much
  pleasure,
I'm tempted to try another in a similar measure :
I refer to the one I wrote on the Baths of Carrycally,
In which I got in about all the rhymes I could rally ; —
For rhymes, as old Hudibras says, the rudders are of
  verses,
By which, like ships at sea, they steer their courses.
(In making this rhyme tho,' I've a notion,
His rudder got damaged some by the stress of the
  ocean.
Perhaps he'd have steered *his* course a little neater,
If he hadn't been pent up in such an uncommon short
  metre.)

Well, to return from this somewhat lengthy digression,

A sort of thing for which I have an extraordinary pre-
    possession

(A tendency, in fact, shared by two large classes, —

Men of real genius, and those sometimes called asses),

T'other morning I clumb up into the Ball of St. Peter,

And should be glad to hammer that out into the same
    free-and-easy metre.

The blue sky was a blue-bell that day, and a bright
    sun was shining,

And the fleecy clouds all turned out to view their sil-
    ver lining.

Old Father March, you see, was the skyey shepherd,

And, every now and then, to be sure, he peppered,

With a big raindrop or two, the hat of a feller

Who happened to venture out without an umbrella ;

But, generally speaking, it must be said in jestice,

He was minding his work up in the Campagna Ce-
    lestis ;

Tending his fleecy flocks, and driving 'em hether and
    thether,

Improving as much as he could the sunny weather,

And letting 'em browse about on any light scud that
    was flying,
So that at night they might keep the Milky Way
    from drying.
So, the morning I speak of, I felt a strong temptátion
To look down on old Rome from an eminent sitiva-
    tion,
Not to speak of the pride felt by human creeturs
In saying they've actilly been up into the Ball of St.
    Peter's.
(I can't think what it is makes this such laborious
    rhyming,
Except a sort of post-presentiment of the labor of that
    climbing.)
Well, as we Yankees say, when we cough to clear our
    vision,
And also by way of making a sort of general transi-
    tion —
(A mighty convenient word that " well," I've often
    found it,
And a *deep well*, too, sometimes, when you come to
    sound it:

I've heerd a feller say nothing but *well* less 'n a hun-
    dred times iu succession,

And every time the word had a different expression) —

But, I declare, all the time I've been rhyming and
    rhyming,

Our party has been climbing and climbing,

Till we're up in that steep narrow stairway, — so
    twisty,

Before you get half-way your head feels misty ;

And *I* felt like a corkscrew working up into the
    throttle

Of a somewhat considerably long inverted bottle.

At last, we stood on the highest floor but one, glad we
    were there ;

And held a council to decide whether the women
    should go any further.

Well, they concluded to stay, and let the lords of cre-
    ation

Carry out their claims to superior elevation.

There was a perpendicular iron ladder, and we men
    clumb it ;

For we were determined to be as near as possible to
    the summit.

We didn't expect to see much through the loop-holes
    of that airy;

But the way the wind sung in that kittle-drum was
    what the natives call *caviare*,

And we Yankees call a *caution :* it was (said an un-
    believer)

As if St. Peter's tympanum, or ear-drum, had got a
    nervous fever,

And was all alive with a kind of prophetic hum-
    ming,

The terrible rumor and roar of a *not* very " good time
    coming."

Well ('tis the fourth time I've uttered this interjec-
    tion),

We came *down*, of course, in the opposite direction

To that in which we'd gone up, stopping a spell to
    admire

A landscape which, as the auctioneers say, " *leaves
    nothing to desire.*"

Only to-day there was one new feature interpolated
    in it,

Which we unfortunately lost by about half a minute :

A young priest, whom, a moment before, we had seen
  engaged in conversation,

Came rushing by us in a good-natured sort of conster-
  nation.

(Imagine, in a similar case, what would·have been
  my feeturs!)

His hat had blown off of the top of St. Peter's!

I felt for him then, though I was an unbeliever:

If his hat could only have been *felt;* but it wa'n't, —
  it was beaver,

And broad-brimmed at that; and the way it must
  have skooted

Down through the air, was a sight with which our
  Ben would have been particularly suited.

Well, (No. 5!) I imagined every kind of fatality

Attending that hat; but how it fared in reality, —

Whether the old black thing came down swooping

Into a flock of sheep, and sent 'em trooping;

Or whether it lodged on a cypress, and sot there,

Like a raven, till folks came round wondering how it
  got there;

Or whether it landed, so to speak, in the river, —
Is more than I yet have beeu able to diskiver.
There are various ways of ending a Poem: miue is, —
When I've said all I have to say, just to add FINIS!

IV.

STRETCHED VERSES.*

WHENEVER you see a fellow driving in a tremendous
    hurry

Through the streets of Rome, holding fast and fierce
    to his Murray,

        Red Murray, —

        Well-read Murray, —

You may be sure he is either a native of Britain,

Or a man from the States (he may be possibly) smitten

With that extraordinary passion some people have for
    doin'

Temple and tomb and church, and every sort of ruin.

Up through the Corso you hear his carriage-wheels
    rattle,

As if he were bound to be in at the death in some
    great battle.

---

* A title borrowed from Jean Paul.

Headlong he goes, as men go in the chase they call
    " steeple,"
At the imminent risk of running over modest peo-
    ple ;
Turning suddenly sharp corners, where the lanes are
    so narrow,
You can hardly drive abreast one wheelbarrow,
And jamming you up so close against the houses,
You fear the hub of the wheel will scrape off your
    flesh or your trousers.
On through the swarm of degenerate moderns he
    dashes,
In his eagerness to get a view of the heroic dust and
    ashes.
Then, when he reaches the spot, he languidly raises
His gold-bowed glass to his eye and gazes,
Crying, " D'yr me ! what an extrornary nation ! "
But, hunger and fatigue having now overcome admi-
    ration,
He jumps into his carriage, feeling as if a boulder
Of pretty considerable size had been rolled off from
    his shoulder.

For, like Cæsar, when he sent that proud report to the
Senate,

" Veni, vidi, vici" (I've been and gone and *done* it),

So when this man goes back to New York, the last
hero,

And tells 'em he's seen the golden house of Nero ;

And the Baths of Caracally and Titus and Domitian

(Or Diocletian), and the house once inhabited by
Titian,

Or Trajan (or somebody else), and the tomb of *Sicily
Mettellar ;*

And the arch of — (plague take it, what's the name of
that feller ?)

Then, as when Dante walked the streets of Florence,

The old women cried with a mixture of admiration
and abhorrence,

" There goes the man who's been down into Hades ! "

So when he goes through his native town, young ladies

Will feel a similar reverence and rapture steal o'er
'em,

As they whisper, " There goes the man who's been in
the Forum ! "

The above lines may seem to some to have been writ-
ten quite at random,

But in fact they're a regular specimen of the style that's
called " tandem."

Tandem means at length, when literally translated,

And I have finished *at length* the task I contemplated.

V.

AN O'ER TRUE TALE.

"ALL WHICH I SAW, AND PART OF WHICH I WAS."

A LOVELY day hung over ancient Rome :
Enrapt I stood, and said :
" Methinks the spirits of the mighty dead
On such a day might have revisited
  Their august home."
But if they had, — ah me !
It would have been to see
Such deeds as ne'er were done
When Vandal, Goth, and Hun,
  With fire and sword
Down on the beauteous city poured ;
As might have tempted the unblushing sun,

For once with shame made red,
To hide his awful head,
Or hurry backward to his ocean-bed.

I stood on holy ground,
Within the Forum's bound,
Where Brutus stood, who could no traitor brook,
And Cicero the spell-bound Senate shook.
But hist! around yon marble slab
What solemn conclave stands in close confab?
With wonder and with awe
One like a priest I saw.
And lady fair,
And man of law, were there.
Why meet they on that temple floor,
Temple of Concord named of yore!
Will they survey and then restore the place
In all its past magnificence and grace?
Or will they haply on the sacred floor
Libations to the goddess Silence pour?
Oh, woe! it is a foul conspiracy
As ever night did see!

I look again, and they are gone!

Was it a dream that fooled my spell-bound eyes?

Ah, no! dead stones have tongues that tell no lies.

Behold! that broken stone,

With its cracked lips, doth mutely speak, and say,

Iu tones too awful for a modern lay:

" Stealers of stone! profane

Diggers in sacred dust! in vain

Shall ye one day call rocks to cover you

From Heaven's avenging view!

Ye that *climb up some other way*, in vain

The heaven of a peaceful miud would gain!

Go, have the sacred marbles wrought

(Which ye by stealth have brought

Beneath your cloaks and other dresses

Wherewith ye sought to cloke your wickednesses)

Iuto the shape of hearts, fit types to be

Of your own marble hearts eternally,

Ye temple-thieves, whose crime

No prose nor rhyme

Is adequate to state," —

Not mine at any rate.

VI.

EVENING CHIMES IN ROME.

(HEARD FROM THE PINCIAN.)

THE evening sun is sinking low
  Behind Mount Mario's graceful line;
And darkly cuts the western glow
  That solitary pine.

And here and there, along the hill,
  I see some lonely cypress stand,
Sombre and spectral, like a still
  Sentinel of the land, —

The holy land, where (the profane,
  Discordant present laid to sleep)
The spirit of the past again
  Its vigils soon shall keep.

See where, against the fading glow,
   Stands black and stark St. Peter's dome,
While, in the valley far below,
   Twinkle the lights of Rome, —

Twinkle as when, on summer nights,
   Here, on the Campus Martius wide,
The fire-flies flashed their fitful lights
   Along the Tiber's tide;

While on the slopes and steeps around
   The moon on marble mansions beamed,
Or many a height, with temples crowned,
   In silvery starlight gleamed.

What changes time and man have made!
   A noisy town this valley fills;
In ruins long ago were laid
   The stately palace-hills.

Thus roll the waves of human life;
   In crested pride they all sweep by:
How soon is hushed their stormy strife!
   They swell and sink and die!

Hark! on my musing, bodeful ear
    What strange, unearthly music swells!
Does my entrancèd spirit hear
    The chime of heavenly bells!

Ah, yes! the requiem-bells are they,
    That knell o'er ages gone to rest,
As vesper-tollings chant how day
    Dies in the fading west.

To the calm land of spirits blest
    They call my restless heart to soar,
Where break thy waves, O human breast!
    And die upon the shore.

To that true " city of the soul,"
    Whose walls and towers shall ne'er decay,
Where man's long yearnings find their goal,
    All shadows flee away!

SIR GEORGE BEAUMONT'S PINE.

[All day long, from my eyrie on the Corso, that lone pine on Mount Mario was the object to which I turned with the greatest interest. One day, I heard it had a history, besides its *natural* history. Years ago, there had stood a group of them on that hill, — special favorites of Sir George. Once, on returning to Rome from an absence in England, he found that the proprietor had cut down all but one, and that the workmen were preparing to fell that. He jumped into his carriage, drove over, bought and saved that one. I have imagined his feelings, in the following parody of our " Woodman, spare that tree! "]

VANDAL, spare that Pine!

Touch not a single bough!

This gold shall make it mine:

No steel shall harm it now.

By Nature's hand 'twas set,

To top this beauteous hill;

That hand preserves it yet,

And shall preserve it still!

That Pine hath been to me

For years a steadfast friend;

And shall I tamely see
   Thy axe its glories end?
Bright Day would spend his gold
   To save that brave old tree!
Its price cannot be told :
   Rash leveller, let it be.

That old familiar tree,
   What rapture of delight
The vision woke in me,
   At morning and at night!
Reflecting morn's fresh beam,
   With mingled love and awe,
And tinged with evening's gleam,
   Its dusky form I saw.

In majesty and grace
   How long that tree hath stood,
With trees of noble race,
   Old monarchs of the wood!
Its brethren all are low,
   Felled by thy cruel hand!
Spare, madman, this last blow,
   And let the old Pine stand!

That glorious old stone-pine,
　　Last gem in Mario's crown,
A king by right divine,
　　And wouldst thou hack it down?
Dearer than Peter's dome
　　To evening's golden sky,
Plume on the brow of Rome,
　　It must not, shall not die!

TO MOUNT MARIO.

I BLESS thee, dear old Mario!
Thee and thy solitary pine:
In morning's flush and evening's glow
How hast thou blest these eyes of mine!
Here on my roof, in day's first beams,
Thou greetest me from thy clear height,
And in the sun's last lingering gleams
Thou smilest me a mute good-night.

I called thee *old*, dear Mario!
For an old friend thou seem'st to me,
As if it had been long ago
My heart first fell in love with thee.
Yet thou art young, my gentle hill,
And ever wilt be young as now,

God's youth and beauty haunt thee still
And shed their radiance on thy brow.

Serene, majestic Mario!
Entranced in evening's hush I stand,
On the north wall of Pincio,
And gaze across the lovely land,
To where, along thy slopes and steeps,
With dark trees fringed and gold light crowned,
Night's solemn shadow slowly creeps,
While vesper chimes float murmuring round.

Then, tender, graceful Mario!
With what admiring love I mark
Thy waving outline's gentle flow
Against the bright West peucilled dark!
It seems as if the glorious land
This very moment had its birth,
As if the great Creator's hand
This very moment shaped the earth.

As if, mysterious Mario!
From God's own pure and teeming soul

Thy line of beauty still did flow
And in sweet undulations roll
Onward and downward, gently down
To fair Janiculum's lower height,
Where Peter's dome, the city's crown,
Dark rises on the glimmeriug night.

Enchanting, lovely Mario!
Thy charms were never limned nor suug
In earthly lines nor tones, — for oh!
No poet's pencil, pen, nor tongue,
Could ever paiut the joy *they* feel
Who look on thee with loving eye,
The raptures from thy breast that steal,
Sweet neighbor of the loving sky.

Hail and farewell, dear Mario!
I bless the hand and bless the hour,
That brought me here to feel the glow
Eukiudled by thy magic power!

Rise, holy hill, for ever rise
Before my mind, when lost to sight,
To lift my spirit to the skies
And bathe my soul in beauty's light.

THE END.